The Flame & The Fallen

The Flame & The Fallen

Dalia Davies

Cover art by Sophie Zuckerman (Twitter: @dextrose_png)

www.daliadavies.com

For anyone given godly reasons to stay
too long in a marriage that failed you.

Content Warnings

Some elements of this book may be triggering to readers. Please see the following list of CWs to ensure that you are comfortable reading this book before you continue.

- Blood
- Bondage (light)
- Death (implied, off page)
- Degradation (light)
- Exhibitionism
- Fluid Kink
- Human/Non-Human Sex
- Polycoria/Trypophobia (brief description)

If you feel anything has been omitted from this list, please let me know at authordaliadavies@gmail.com or using the contact form at www.daliadavies.com

I do what the good girls don't.

- Elle King

See You in Hell

The sun dips low in the sky and the city that sits over the pit of Hell starts to ease some of that restless energy it has held all day.

All Hallows Eve is upon us and the unwed adults of the city await their judgement.

Sinner or saint.

I sit alone in my one-bedroom apartment, staring out at the horizon as I twist the heart locket on my bracelet and take deep breaths. My foot taps incessantly and I don't try to still it.

There is no question of what my fate will be: *Sinner.*

The arrest warrant they've waited to serve isn't the reason I'll join the others on the Devil's dance floor tonight. It's a different piece of paper that has given my soul into the Devil's keeping tonight—and for the next year, if no saint should kiss me.

The warrant means I'm damned if they do. The divorce decree means I'm damned if they don't.

Smoothing down the skirt of my dress, I wonder if I shouldn't change. The demand for funereal black is a tradition, but why follow the rules now when I've already broken so many of them?

If the Devil cares that my dress is blue, he can change it.

Perhaps, if he confronts me himself, I'll issue my own list of complaints.

They are accusations I should lay at the feet of God, but she never leaves her Heaven. And I will never see the pearly gates.

Cursed simply by being born to a family trapped here by God's cruel benevolence, I can't run away from this fate.

Her rules are strictly lined out for those of us whose forebears were created in Eden and held back when Adam and Eve were cast out.

Paradise comes with iniquitous punishments. But this city is not the Garden and the fruit of knowledge has long since rotten away.

A chirp from the table beside me draws my attention and I take another deep breath before I pick up the phone. Despite knowing better, I read the admonishing text there.

I can hear her voice as I do. I can imagine the sobbing with her pleas.

She's already lost one daughter to the Devil's dance. I am still surprised my mother hasn't burst through my door with a priest and some unwitting sacrifice in tow.

A simple "I do" would save me from one fate—so many others have wed this day to save themselves.

But perhaps I deserve a year toiling under the Devil's watch.

Holy matrimony can't save me anymore.

I bought this dress the day the paperwork was finalised.

Niro has already remarried—a woman barely a year older than our daughter—and knowing that he will not be on the dance floor tonight is a faint solace.

Breaking our holy union put me on the list of sinners to dance for the Devil tonight.

I wonder if Niro has already been unfaithful to the girl he convinced to save him. I wonder if she only used him to save herself.

His philandering won't take him to Hell tonight. God cares only that he is faithful to her.

I watch the sun finally dip below the horizon and the scent of brimstone fills the air and a great crack echoes around me. I fall into the pit, landing on the glassy black surface of the dance floor. And, eyes wide, I look at the others around me. It's been more than twenty years since I've danced at this masquerade. And then, I was with the saints.

Tonight, the sinners all look the same. Only a saint would need to see their disguises.

Like me, each of them wears a cage around their head. Manacles and chains move us like marionettes if we do not dance on our own. And when one swirls past me, dancing with a man in a black suit, I can see why my mouth won't open.

Dark threads stitch our lips closed.

The next who passes has torn theirs open, bleeding as they silently scream.

I am one of hundreds of other sinners, waiting for a saint's kiss.

I may be the only one unsure if I want it.

Music echoes in my bones and the first saint deposited into my arms eyes me warily. She doesn't know that I am not the devil I'm disguised as.

There are too few saints and too many sinners. And the woman in my arms breaks free of me, twirling herself into the arms of another sinner. He strains toward her, silently begging for the kiss that will save him and transport them both back to the city far above our heads.

Another saint spins into my arms. He is a mere boy, possibly only eighteen, and I recoil from him when he leans close.

He abandons me, too.

The first saint and sinner disappear in a dark puff as I twirl around the room and saints flit between dance partners. Very few sinners will find their way home tonight.

Something high on the walls of the pit draws my attention away from the saints. A faint glimmer of gold in the firelight.

But the dark spectator is neither the Devil nor a sinner... and they certainly are no saint.

Devil or Angel

Three more partners pass me to the next, and I barely catch a glimpse of their faces. The dark and glimmering presence has so fully trapped my attention that I watch it through every turn and dip. The chains that move me require little to no participation from me.

If not for the golden shroud they wear, I might not have seen them at all. Black skin, veined with thin lines of gold, like marble, and wings that faintly glimmer.... They blend in with the stones of the wall behind them.

I'm certain they don't belong here. They are a creature of Heaven, not one of Hell.

I can't see their face in the dark shadow of that shroud, but I *feel* it the moment their gaze locks on me. It feels as though I've been dipped into a pool of sparkling water and I shiver, spooking the latest saint and sending them fleeing.

They leave me without a partner, and the creature descends on me, scooping me into their arms and turning on deft feet as their wings draw close.

"You are a pretty little thing," they say, dark fingers taking hold of the cage around my head and with a twist of their wrist, it bursts in a shimmering cloud like glitter. The remnants fall to the floor and climb up the blue fabric of my dress in trails of stars.

The cage is gone, the manacles too, but my lips are still sewn shut. They haven't freed me. They've simply captured me for their own.

"What is your name, sweet creature?" They ask.

All I can do is shake my head.

A low rumble echoes from the inside of the hood of their shroud and they raise their hand, brushing the back of their knuckles over my cheek and then drawing their thumb across my lips.

The sutures that held my mouth closed dissolve beneath that touch and I draw in a long and shaky breath, licking my lips and wondering at the velvety softness covering them like the silkiest lipstick.

"You shine too brightly to be mistaken for the lord of darkness. I thought you were a star when I first saw your flame." They tip my head back and their hand draws down my neck, their fingers wrapping about my throat. "What is your name?"

"Thea." I whisper it, but I know they hear me.

"Woman of god... how strange then, to find you here." They chuckle and lean close, the feather-soft fabric of their shroud brushing my cheek. "That cunt will abandon anyone who isn't willing to play by the rules of her asinine game."

I blink up at them, trying to remember the last time I heard anyone call God a cunt.

It would have been my little sister.

That memory makes me turn back to the dancers. I search among them and find her twirling in the arms of the Devil himself.

And I move myself so that she can't see me.

I don't know why.

I should flee from the creature who has me trapped in their arms. I should go to her and the safety of family.

But that fizzing sensation still flutters over my skin. And some magnetism holds me to them.

I look up at them, into the darkness of their shroud, but not trying to see their face beyond that impenetrable veil.

"Who are you?"

Their response is faint laughter and then, "Have you perchance heard the name Zuriel?"

I sort through my memories from my childhood education and the angel names my mother made me memorise decades ago. "The archangel of virtue?"

"I am he."

We turn around the room, dancing with the others, but at the furthest edges of the floor.

Even still, when we get close to Keres, I turn my face to keep myself out of sight.

"Why do you hide from the Devil and his dame?"

I look at them again, blissfully unaware of me, so wrapped up in each other... Keres spent years searching him out. She found her Devil and I've no doubt she's fucked him, too. She is not a coward.

I swallow back the admission of who she is to me and look up at Zuriel clenching my jaw tight.

"Now, that *is* interesting." I can hear the smile in his voice, though I can't see it.

"You don't need to tell me your secrets." He says it as though he knows he'll learn them on his own. "But you do need to answer a question."

I swallow back the instant instinct to tell him I don't need to do anything. I want to know what the question is.

"Do you deserve to be here?"

"Yes." There is no point in lying.

His head tips to the side and the shroud moves, but not enough to see his face. "What did you do to deserve damnation?"

I repeat his words back to him, "I don't need to tell you my secrets."

It feels as though there is a warm glow on my face as he leans closer. "No, you do not. Can I tell you one of mine?"

"Yes."

"I deserve to be here, too."

He kisses me and when he draws back, everything around us has turned blue. The flames, the walls, the glittering barrier of the broken ceiling far overhead....

We've stopped dancing, and he steps back, over the threshold of a dark hallway and holds out his hand. "Will you come find absolution with me, Thea?"

Be Not Afraid

I place my hand in his and when he pulls me into that dark corridor with him, a different shiver slides down my skin, like I've shed it the way a snake does.

"Come away from here before the Devil notices you're missing."

He turns me into his arms and dances me down the corridor, never letting my feet touch the ground, but then again, his don't touch it either.

I can't count the number of wings sprouting from his back. They're constantly moving. They keep us just far enough off the ground and always moving slowly forward.

Tipping my chin up, he brushes his fingers along my face. "I can keep you here as long as you do everything I say."

"Is that a threat?" It doesn't feel like one, even though it should.

"Maybe." He tips his head to the side and the shroud moves, exposing the hard planes of his chest. I don't touch it, even though I want to. "The rules of Hell aren't kind."

We twirl into the transept of a cathedral cluttered with debris, its floor flooded with mirror-clear water.

He leads me past the choir stalls and I tip my head back. I have to in order to see the broken statue of an angel that fills the space beneath the enormous stained glass windows of the apse.

"Where are we?"

"The Devil's palace is a hundred angelic cathedrals crashed into each other. When he fell, she sent these places with him. This one was mine."

Lifting his hand, he points to the marks carved into the wall high above and the murals painted on the walls.

His name is there, in languages I shouldn't be able to read, but I know that's what they say.

We stop at the altar, at the feet of the broken statue... a statue of him.

"Are you willing to obey me, starlight? Will you do anything I say?"

I'm already damned. What could he do to me that is worse than what would wait for me with the rest of the sinners?

Perhaps I hesitate too long.

One warm finger presses to the tip of my chin and lifts my face up to him. "You always have a choice. Stay with me and play with me... or don't. I won't turn you out into the hellish wastes. You may hide in these halls as long as you can. But he will, eventually, catch you and cast you out."

"But you'll keep me safe?"

"I promise you'll enjoy everything I make you do."

Obedience. That was what everyone has ever asked of me: my parents, God, my ex-husband....

"And if I say yes and then don't obey?"

"Then you won't receive your reward."

My reward. *Not* a punishment.

I glance down.

I can't help myself.

"Is that what you want for your reward, sweet mortal?"

I swallow back the denial. That is what I should say. In this moment, I don't want to lie anymore.

My sister was brave enough to fuck the Devil.

I may not be as wicked, but with the delights of Heaven in reach....

"Yes." I want it very badly.

Down on Your Knees to Pray

"You are a sinner, are you not, Thea?"

I nod.

"Then be a good girl." He brushes his fingers over my throat, holding it for a fraction of a second before he moves and all my muscles tense... wanting. "Get on your knees to pray for mercy."

I blink at him for a half a heartbeat and then I comply, almost without thought.

My dress bunches beneath my knees, saving me from the hard and sharp stones.

"God can't hear prayers down here. And even if she could, the cunt sent you here. She's not going to rescue you."

"Are you?"

His laughter is low and mirthless. "I can't even rescue myself, starlight. These wings aren't powerful enough to get us back into Heaven."

"Zuriel isn't one of the fallen angels." And this is Hell. It could be a lie, a demon's trick.

"The accuracy of that statement is based on timing. Zuriel *wasn't* one of the fallen, and yet, time reveals us all to be sinners under her hypocrisy and false promises. Once I was the angel of virtue. Perhaps now, with your help, I will be the angel of vice."

"If not to God, who then should I pray to?"

Dark hand dragging along the front of his shroud, Zuriel draws it open, revealing a cock that is more than perfectly placed... it is heavenly. More black marble, *thickly* veined with gold.

I lick my lips and then force myself to look away, to look back up at the face I cannot see.

"Would you like to worship at my altar?"

It's a question, not a command, and I swallow back my trepidation.

It's been years since I've done anything like that. But if an angel offers, how could I decline?

Because Niro told you you sucked. And not in a good way.

But I had never *wanted* to suck his cock. There's something perversely tantalising about Zuriel's.

I take hold of him and he fits perfectly in my hand.

Maybe it's because I'm already in Hell that feels like tacit permission to do all of the things I was told I never should.

Don't *want*, don't do, don't be....

But I do and I will and I am.

He's warm on my tongue. The taste of him is soft, though nothing else is.

And he fits in me like he knew the shape of me already.

"You were beautiful before, but on your knees, with my cock in your mouth, I've never met another creature who could compare, sweet starlight."

A voice whispers in my mind, "*He'd say that to anyone on their knees for him.*"

I shove it away. I don't care if it's my position, not my person that elicits those words, I let them sink into my skin and bleed into my veins and let my eyes flutter closed as I work myself onto his cock, relaxing my jaw to take as much of him as possible.

I fall into a rhythm, rocking against him, and it makes me long to be filled again. It's been years since I've been wanted. I didn't realise how much I craved it.

His hands smooth into my hair, clasping my head and taking control, making me slow. "I did not expect you would be so hungry... you should not have been neglected for so long."

I cannot answer him, and he doesn't withdraw to allow it.

"You were made to worship by a God whose love is conditional. Always made to give if you ever wished to receive. But you are at my altar now and you will worship by receiving."

One hand spreads in my hair and he takes complete control.

My hands drop to his hips, needing to steady myself as he fucks my mouth, sweetly at first, and then in a way that makes me moan around him.

I want to take all of him. I want to make him come before he expects it.

This had always been an act of contrition before. A box to be checked off.

Sucking Zuriel's cock... I would worship this way forever if given the chance.

I force my jaw wider and the tip of him brushes the back of my throat, making it spasm. But his hand moves down to my throat and the gagging sensation is gone.

Swallowing, my throat works on him, fully invading me, and he chuckles.

"You are going to drink me down, sweet starlight. You'll swallow my cum like it's nectar, and you are a glutton."

He comes a moment later, warmth flooding my tongue and then my throat. Eyes wide, I meet his, drinking down as much of him as I'm able. Exactly as he said.

My mouth is so full, I can't swallow any more without choking and when his grip loosens on my hair and he draws himself from me, the excess spills from my lips, down my chin and onto my breasts.

"I was wrong," he says, brushing his thumb over my lower lip. "You were beautiful before, but now, painted with my cum, you are utterly breathtaking."

When he releases my chin, I drop my head, trying to catch my breath, and I see the aftermath.

Golden streaks stain my decolletage, disappearing beneath the blue bodice of my dress. The path of his cum is gilded into my skin.

I touch my chin and feel nothing but skin, but I know I've been marked by him, whether he meant for it to happen or not.

Taking my hand, he draws me to standing. "A bit of your starlight has started to shine through. Let's see if we can make you glow."

Hooking that hand in the front of my dress, he pulls it from me, fully intact, and tosses it over the choir stalls behind him.

He lifts me, setting me atop the altar that is clean and smooth despite looking as though it's recently been on fire.

"Will you let me taste your goodness, Thea? Will you let me devour you whole if I wish?"

I swallow back the tremor of fear in my throat and nod. "Yes."

"You will do as I say—"

He isn't done, but, "Yes."

The rest of the question fades to silence.

"You belong to me now, Thea. Until you take yourself back, you are mine. Do you understand me?"

"I do."

He reaches up and brushes his thumb over my cheek. "Good girl. And what will you say to reclaim yourself?"

"I won't."

"Only fools give themselves no escape. And you are not a fool."

There is only one word I can be certain I wouldn't say without meaning to. "Niro."

"You would invoke the name of another man?"

"It's something I won't accidentally say while..."

He kisses my knee. "And if I make you forget his name entirely?"

"Then we'll come up with another word."

"He stifled you, didn't he?"

"Yes." He doesn't ask *who* Niro was.

"Men like that do not deserve gifts like you." He reaches into his shroud and from the darkness he pulls out the glowing circlet of his halo, so dim.

He must see the question in my eyes. "There is little light left in me. But you..." He touches it to my skin and it flares bright. "You can make it shine."

His voice is a dark whisper in my ear. "I don't want to snuff your flame. I want to make you burn." He places the halo on my head, slipping it down to cover my eyes and lays me back.

The light is so bright it feels like it bleeds into me, even though I keep my eyes screwed shut. But I open them on a gasp a moment later.

The faintest tickling draws across my skin—feathers.

The whisper of the touch makes me flinch away from it even as I arch toward it.

He draws it down my leg and across my mound and I clench as it passes over my aching pussy.

I want to reach for him, but I keep my fists tightly balled.

Zuriel is in charge. He can do what he wishes with me, and even if I want more than he'll give, I think I'm going to enjoy every moment of it—even the wanting.

His finger follows after the feather, drawing down the line of me and then back up to circle my clit. "I don't think this little mortal pussy is ready for my cock yet."

I whimper, wanting to disagree.

"Do you think it could survive my tongue?"

I want to find out.

"Yes. Please." The words are a hoarse whisper as he pinches my clit and I jerk, even as I try to hold perfectly still.

"There's no one here to deny yourself for." His grip tightens on my thigh and he moves my legs, settling me so that my knees fall open and I know I'm on garish display. "No one here to see how divinely you were created, but me."

His tongue finds my clit, lapping once. "God may not have known it, but she created you *for* me. Should I fly back to the gates and thank one cunt for another?"

"No, don't stop."

His chuckle is soft and heavy against my skin and then his lips lock onto my clit, sucking once, painfully and pleasurably sharp, and I can't stand it anymore.

I cry out and faint wings flutter in the distant vaults, dust shimmers down on me, and Zuriel chuckles, soft breath against my skin.

"The angelic choirs don't compare to the beauty of that sound, starlight."

Angelic Hosts

Zuriel slips the halo from my head and I blink away the dark lines left behind.

He watches me, twirling the bright ring on his finger. "I like that bright eyed look. Maybe you truly are a star, not a mortal at all."

Lifting me down, he leans close and the shroud flutters against my cheek as lips I haven't seen brush my ear. "What sins did you commit to send you here, I wonder?"

"Are you musing? Or is that an actual question you want me to answer?"

"You may keep your secrets... for now." He draws his finger along my stomach and I flinch as he traces the scarred remnants of my children's entrance into this world. "I do wonder, though, what happened to your holy matrimony?"

When he meets my eyes, I wait for the command, but he doesn't make me tell him any of my secrets.

"You are old enough that you knew what awaited you, and you're beautiful enough you could have saved yourself from the Dance. But you're here." He tips his head to the side and then, finger beneath my chin, he draws me forward, brushing his lips across mine, but he doesn't kiss me.

I stare into the darkness of that shroud, and the pinpricks of gold that make me think of the reflection of eyes... so many eyes.

"Tell me why you're here, Thea." He toys with the locket on my wrist.

I swallow, expecting some kind of compulsion. But I don't *have* to tell him. I imagine he'd know if I lied, but I *could* lie. There's a choice here....

But I won't deceive him.

"I came to find my sister."

"Did you?" He holds his hand out and the dress floats to him, dancing as if it has wings of its own.

Pressing the fabric against my skin, he slides it onto me —through me—as if it had never left.

"That would be dangerous." He twists a finger in my hair. "Step foot outside this palace and the damned will try to devour you."

"She's not out there. She's in here," I say, and then use the same words he used when we danced. "She's the Devil's Dame."

"That is even more dangerous." He scoops me up into his arms and, with a flutter of his wings, we move down the nave. "You're not supposed to be here, starlight."

We wind through a maze of halls and when he stops, feet touching the floor again, it is at a channel cut into the floor where the water pours over to sizzle on dark rocks below. The steam reaching up like ghostly hands.

"This is the boundary of where you are safe." Everything on this side of the channel is tinted blue, even the fire that licks outside the windows. Everything on the other is red.

Heat flutters across my skin from that side.

"I have to speak to the Devil." The words are grudging, but he kisses me and my knees go weak. "Explore if you must, but I can't protect you if you cross this boundary. Stay close and if they find you, *run*."

He leaves me and when I'm no longer in his arms, I sink to the floor, my legs like jelly. I stay there for longer than I expected, trying to find my wits as the water flows around me. I want to lie on the floor and fall into the spinning delirium that washes through me. But I should find Keres.

I can't hide in these safe halls, no matter how tempting it may be.

When I hop over that channel, dark hands reach for my feet, but they only manage to grab my shoes and tear the hem of my dress.

I fall to the floor and immediately struggle up. The stones are baking, the air is too close. Everything here hurts, if only just a little.

But I've dealt with pain all my life. A little more to get to my sister won't kill me.

Putting the Arch in Archangel

I shouldn't be surprised when Zuriel finds me before I've tracked down Keres. The Devil's palatial cathedral has too many rooms to explore, too many hallways to get lost down.

One moment I'm alone, the next, wings brush my arms and he's behind me.

"Didn't find what you were looking for, did you, starlight?" He wraps one arm around my waist and draws me back against him fully. The other drags up my the line of my skirt, the fabric there opening like there was always a slit up my thigh.

"An hour in Hell can feel like eternity..." His hand flickers along the inside of my thigh and his fingers delve into my pussy.

"You are dripping with anticipation." Teeth graze my ear. "Is that how badly you want to be fucked? Are you wet at the idea of this sacrilege?"

"I'm wet for the idea of you."

"I shouldn't take you here. It isn't safe."

"Do it anyway."

"If that is your wish." He holds me tighter and I gasp as he lifts me, flying upward until we're hidden by the shadows in the ribbed vaulting so far overhead.

There, he lays me across one, stomach to stone, head and legs dangling on either side.

I grip the stone tight, swallowing the startled scream that wants to fly free.

"Hold tight, starlight. You don't want to fall."

Trapped as I am on my belly, my breasts press forward, falling out of the neck of my dress. He flips the skirt behind me up and tosses it over my back, but it doesn't cover my head like it should.

I'd almost rather be naked. When his hands smooth over my skin and his lips caress their way along my thighs, I *know* I'd rather be naked.

I tug at it with a whimper. "Please—"

The request is lost on my next breath.

"If you wish for something, you must ask for it."

"I want this gone."

His fingers twist in the lacings at my back and he pulls. I don't move, but the dress is gone.

Pulled straight through me, I watch it as it falls to the floor, fluttering and floating away to land on the tiles below.

I lose all sight of it when Zuriel strokes me and my eyes flutter closed.

"What else do you want?" He asks, fingers playing with me, tips dipping inside to spread me open and caress me. "I could take what I want, but I learned from the best. I'm going to make you beg for it."

He already knows I will.

"But unlike that cunt, I'll let you have it. Eventually."

"I want..." I take a deep breath. The words are something

I shouldn't say. Desires are something I've been trained to hide. "I want to be fucked."

"Such a simple request." He muses, and I look back at him over my shoulder. "And an unnecessary one, starlight. I was going to fuck you one way or another. The question is *how*?"

Everything is still so hot, but a cold slither trails down my spine.

"Any way you want. I'm yours, remember?"

"That doesn't mean you don't get a say."

"I don't know what to ask for."

His fingers dig into my hips like claws.

"How long has it been since someone has opened you up and taken their fill of you?"

Decades. "A while."

"I've tasted you. I know the sweet flavour of your pussy. I see how it weeps for me now." His hands sweep over me. "How is it possible someone had this so close and chose to let your love fizzle and die?"

I don't want to answer him and he doesn't make me. "Some aren't prepared to pay the price for a woman as exquisite as you. He'll sour for the new wife, too. She will grow cold for him as you did. Men like that have patterns, they work in cycles. You cut a straight path. One that led you to me."

"It was before him." I say. "The last time someone fucked me the way I hope you will."

"That is more than a while."

I pull in a sharp breath as he notches his cock against me, and I moan as he slides into my wet and wanting pussy.

"We'll have to see which path your punishment takes."

He works me open, coaxing me all the while, reminding me to hold on to the ribbing.

"I wish you could see what I see," He says as he draws back from me once more. "I wish you knew how greedy your pussy is for me. I know you can feel the way it holds on and doesn't want to let go, but if you could *see* the way your body wants to keep me."

"I would keep you if I could." I whisper the words to the stone, but he hears them. If I could sling my legs up over the ribbing, I would. I want to open myself to him, to give myself to him and let him take every part of me until there is nothing left.

His next thrust is brutal and I draw in a sharp breath that squeaks in my throat, echoing away from us.

"Hush, starlight. We're still within the Devil's reach. Scream, and he may appear to take you away from me."

But Zuriel doesn't go easy on me. His next thrust knocks my hips against the vaulting, and I squeeze my eyes shut and hold more tightly to the stone.

With each press of his hips, I feel even closer to falling.

I want to rock back against him. I want to play my part in this fuckery, but he doesn't let me and I can get no leverage, slung over the rib as I am.

The next sound I make dies half way out of my mouth, like a hiccup.

"That's right. Silence or I'll stop. Is that what you want?"

"No." I whisper the word, and still it rings too loudly. But I swallow the next sound, pressing my palm to my mouth, sacrificing stability for silence.

"I love how easily you've learned to obey." The pressure makes me gasp as he presses a long finger into my ass. "I will take you in every divine way before I am satisfied."

"I haven't—"

"Good." He pulses his finger. "This belongs to me, like the rest of you."

I nod, agreeing as the combination of pressures and the air sweeping across my slick skin from his wings threatens to undo me. He fucks me like I belong completely to him and his possessive words wrap around me like a spell.

My orgasm sneaks up on me, but I can't be wholly surprised as writhe and jerk against his hold. As I screw my eyes and mouth so tightly shut that it's like Hell no longer exists around us.

He thrusts into me one last time and his body jerks against mine.

And when he's finished and he withdraws from me, golden cum drips down my legs, droplets falling to splash and sizzle on the dark tiles below.

By Faith Alone

He releases me and I don't have the energy to hold on anymore... but as the air flutters around me, he catches me, holding me tightly to him.

"You don't get to hurt yourself, starlight. You are mine now. And my things are precious."

Scooping up my dress, he cradles me close and flies back to the halls where the light turns everything blue. He flies us up a spiralling tower in the centre of an enormous vaulted room, and when he alights through an arched window that has no glass.

"Do angels need bedrooms?"

He chuckles as he lays me on the feather-soft mattress. "Angels need nothing. At least, that's what the cunt told us. But a long time ago, creatures like me saw the way that she doted on creatures like you and wanted to know what that might be like.

"So we grew limbs and attempted to make faces. We created homes for ourselves that we hadn't needed before. And do you know what?"

I swallow, shaking my head, not daring to speak.

"The cunt still didn't care about us enough to notice what we'd done until Lucifer—once her favourite—got tired of the way she neglected the rest of us."

"And he fell."

"So the story says."

"And you came with him?"

The laugh that echoes from his shroud is bitter.

"No. I was a fool and stayed long after I should have known that she was never going to care for her angels again. She's started to lose interest in humans and when she finally moves on to something that will hold her interest, it will not be by coming back to us."

Once again, he plucks his halo from the darkness, drawing it through the fabric of the shroud. But he doesn't blindfold me this time.

He wraps the warm band around my wrist, tangling with my bracelet and clinking against the locket. It flares as it shrinks until I'm manacled. "Will you do anything I say?"

"I already told you, yes."

"Good girl." He flicks his finger tips and my hands fly above my head, hooking on some unseen tether and it lifts me into the air, dangling me a bare inch above the floor.

When I look back at him, he presses a finger to my lips. "Be silent."

I expect some form of punishment, or perhaps a new type of play, but he turns his back on me, walking across the room to an enormous chair.

He sits, fanning his wings out behind him and for a moment, all I can do is stare. There is something so beautiful in the shape of him, I hold my breath, afraid that any unnecessary movement of the air will make him disintegrate and disappear like dust.

Maybe this *is* my personal hell.

Just like up above, the things I want are out of reach and never really mine.

He watches me as the silence stretches on and after a time—when I've forced myself to breathe, despite my silly notions—I think I might be able to see his face.

"Who were you before you danced?" He asks when the silence has grown almost painful.

I almost answer him, but it was a question, not a command. And he told me to stay silent.

He watches me from behind that shroud and I wish I could see his face. I wish I could tell if he was smiling or if he disapproved of the obedience I've chosen.

When he speaks again, there is an amusement in the command. "Tell me who you were before you danced." Again, it's my choice to comply.

"I was a daughter, a sister, a mother...."

"But not a wife?"

"Not anymore." He knows that. And he knows that I'm divorced. I wouldn't be here if I was still married, or if Niro had had the decency to die.

Golden threads slide down from where my hands were tied and twist around my ankles before they walk me to him like a marionette.

"I would have come to you if you asked," I say.

"I know."

Those golden threads loosen, but they haven't brought me close enough.

When I move, the invisible force holding my hands over my head moves with me and I take another step forward and then I place one knee beside his leg.

"Is that what you want?" He asks, pulling the sides of his shroud apart and showing me his golden-veined cock once more.

"Yes."

I use the halo to steady myself as I straddle him fully, but his hand goes to my hip and he holds me there, hovering over him.

"This beautiful gold stained pussy is still mine, isn't it?" He runs his thumb along me before raising it to his lips and sucking it clean.

"Yes."

"Do you want to say his name?"

"No." I never want to say it—to think it—again.

His grip loosens on me and I sink onto him.

He watches the place where our bodies join, and I watch the darkness where his face should be.

"That's right. Go slowly."

I don't remind him that I've done this before. I'm not that woman anymore. I haven't been her for close to twenty years.

His commands caress my skin like the softest feathers.

"You watch me like you think I'll sprout horns and reveal some trickery."

"I want to see your face."

"You don't."

"Do you think you'll frighten me? Or is seeing you a sin? As you can see, sins don't frighten me."

"Is this a sin, starlight?"

"How could it be? Angels can't sin."

He tips his head back and even though I can't see his face, I know he's looking at my bound wrists. "Haven't you noticed? I've traded my halo to have you."

As if saying the word released it from the invisible grip over my head, that support vanishes.

My wrists are still bound together, and Zuriel guides them down, wrapping my arms around his neck.

His hand slides up my spine, tangling in my hair and he pulls me to him, kissing me as all of my other senses vanish, leaving only touch behind.

The shroud that veils his face makes it impossible to see, the thundering of my heart makes it impossible to hear....

And even though I'm on top of him and should be able to take some control, I have none.

Zuriel moves me and moulds me to his liking. He fucks me as if I do truly belong to him—as if I'm a toy he'd be fully within his rights to break.

He suckles my nipple and bites at the flesh of my breasts.

His fingers dig into my ribs and he whispers dark angelic words against my skin.

"I should bind you up tight, starlight. Keep you for my own and seal shut your mouth so you can never relinquish my control. I would give up Heaven a hundred times over for it."

His thumb swirls and tweaks my clit and when his lips go to my neck, kissing and biting. I'm done for.

I arch back on a scream as I come and he lets me fall, but I don't come off of him. I don't land on the floor. I hit the soft surface of a bed and he kneels below me, raising my hips so that he can fuck me in a way I can see.

His cock disappears into me, the golden veins looking molten, slick from my cum.

"Do you see how your body wants me?"

It's not just my body that wants him. "Yes."

"I will give you what it wants—what you want—every chance I get.

He pulls out of me, spraying cum on my thighs and belly in bright splashes.

"You are mine," he says with a musing hum as he draws shapes in the slick gold he's left on my stomach. "And I don't think I'll let you go."

Sinning for Sainthood

The bed is shrouded in burnt velvet curtains and they flutter in a silent breeze as Zuriel lays beside me, tracing the splattered patterns of gold across my skin and feeding me morsels of some divine treat that fills me like a full meal.

"Tell me what sin put you in a devil's disguise last night."

I almost ask him if he'd rather move to a confessional booth. I'm sure the ruins of one exist here.

But even though the words are soft, they're still a command.

That's why I don't avoid the question. "I killed a man."

"Do you regret it?"

Everything I was taught as a child tells me I should be, but.... "No."

"Why?"

Answering that isn't simple.

"When my sister didn't return—when she claimed her Devil—I found a list she left behind. Names of people who used heavenly loopholes to avoid both God and the Devil's punishments. People who shortly thereafter disappeared.

And then more names who weren't on her list... the pattern was easy to see once I knew it existed.

"Keres took care of them. But they were the obvious ones. Others slipped through the cracks. One such person fell into my path, so I took care of it."

"Vengeance is mine, I will repay." Zuriel chuckles beneath his breath. "You took that vengeance away from her, *that* is the sin. The cunt doesn't like when others do her job for her. It makes her look lazy." He traces the gilded line across my décolletage and says. "It's no surprise you are as vengeful as your sister. She doesn't like me much."

My muscles tense, but I force myself to relax. "You've seen my sister?"

"The little fool is happy with her Devil." He traces his fingers down the side of my face and I shiver at the touch. "I wonder...."

But whatever he was about to say, he keeps it to himself. And it's my turn to ask a question.

"What made you leave Heaven?"

"What made me abandon the heavenly hosts and find may way here just in time to claim you? That is a story too long for tonight."

"Is it night?"

He ignores that question completely. "The simplest version of the answer is that God is a cunt. It took me too long to understand that there is no redeeming someone who believes *they* are the redeemer."

His hand trails lower, I flinch as his fingers pass over the scar on my stomach and I shiver when they slip between my legs.

"Would you like to try to be my salvation? Would you like to drain me of my sins and cleanse me with your cries of pleasure?"

"Is that how it works?"

"Maybe not. But we could try it."

I would have laughed, but all I can do is moan when he parts me and his fingers probe and swirl.

My eyes are squeezed shut when a fluttering sound moves the air around me, and then, he settles between my legs. "This is the holiest of communions."

His mouth finds my pussy again and his tongue... I have no idea what shape it is, only that it can't resemble a human one. There's too much of it and it moves in ways I can't describe. It reaches places I didn't know existed. I shudder as it fills me and toys with my clit at the same time.

I squirm and arch and spread my legs wider, needing him to fill me as deeply as possible.

"Please." The word is a whisper, as if the empty feeling inside of me is trying to suck me down into the darkness.

"Please what, starlight?"

"Please use me as your salvation."

He chuckles lowly and for a moment, I wonder if he isn't an angel, but a demon meant to destroy every last thread of godly virtue I have.

I'm already damned and I wouldn't despair if he was.

He flips me over onto my stomach and smooths his hands down my sides until he reaches my ass. "This pussy wants to be filled, but I think I'll feast on your other delights."

He palms my cheeks and spreads me open as he speaks.

"I'm going to fuck this divine little asshole until you beg me to never leave it." He leans down, kissing the base of my spine. "I'll hollow out a place inside of you and make it my own."

"I've never..." A second time, the words catch in my throat as he caresses me.

"Not even with that husband who failed you?"

I shake my head against the sheets.

"Say his name if you want this to stop."

I bite my tongue, because I don't.

He kisses my shoulder this time and leans close to whisper. "I'm not going to hurt you. But I won't be gentle either."

Nodding, I swallow back the nervous burble of laughter.

"Why didn't you let your husband do this?"

I stare straight ahead, I can't look back at him. I can't look at myself. "Because by the time he demanded it, I already knew about the affairs."

"And to think, that was *holy* matrimony." He trails a finger down my spine. "He will get what he's due when he finds his way here in the end. But I'll give you your punishment and your reward now."

Cool liquid drips onto me, pooling exactly where it needs to go, and he works me open with his fingers and then his tongue and I twist my hands in the sheets, burying my face in the cool fabric.

My breath tangles in my throat and I screw my eyes shut.

"Relax, starlight." But as he says it, pressure opens me as he slides the tip of himself into me. "Breathe."

I do. The shaky sound feels like a betrayal. The fact that it helps makes me feel foolish.

"Touch yourself, starlight." He eases back, rocking against me. "Play with yourself while I make room for myself within you."

He presses deeper into me, as I slide my fingers through the curls on my mound and coat them in the wetness from my empty, and aching pussy.

That first contact with my pussy makes me clench down on him. But it helps more than it hurts, and I moan into the mattress as he works me open, as his cock stretches me.

Each thrust makes me want to squirm away and press back to meet them at the same time.

I want to be full of him, completely.

And when he's eased himself all the way into me, testing me twice before his hands grip my hips in a brutal grasp, he says. "It's okay if you want to scream. This far away, the Devil will assume you're one of the damned."

My eyes fly wide and my mouth drops open on a silent gasp as that grip drags me back onto him with his next, brutal thrust.

Holy fuck.

My hand leaves my clit, tangling in the sheets as I try to gain back some control over the movement of my body, and I do scream, but not from pain.

It should hurt. He fucks me like he wants to break me. He fucks me like I exist only for his pleasure.

But it doesn't hurt.

If this is Hell, what would have awaited me in Heaven?

My scream turns into a sob of pleasure and I plead with him. Not for mercy or restraint, or even release.

Harder. Yes. More.

My vocabulary has been decimated of all other words.

His hand is the one that finds my clit this time and he's no less brutal to it. The rough, swirling pressure, the jerking movements.

"Come for me with my cock in your ass, starlight. I want to feel you strangle it as your pleasure rocks through you. I want to hear my names on your golden lips and I want you to beg me—"

What he wants me to beg, I don't hear. This scream is so loud, it feels as though it should have shattered the windows high above us. And I don't bury the sound in a pillow or my hand. I let it ring through the room. I let it echo off the walls.

I want all of the demons and the damned to know how well he fucks me.

I want him to know how much I crave it.

Telling him is impossible. My throat aches from that strangled scream and I don't trust it to convey the words.

Lips on my shoulder, Zuriel kisses me as he fucks me. He whispers against my skin and both words and lips brand me in different ways.

And then, his grip tightens, he lifts away from me, and I cry out, wanting to demand he come back and fill me again.

But the warmth of his cum seeps into my skin and I collapse forward, eyes too heavy.

He holds me close to him, lips on my forehead. "I wonder if a star could be as happy here as a fool is...."

I fall asleep as he traces a feather along the new lines his golden cum has left along my spine.

Divine Damnation

My eyes flutter open to the sound of crashing in the distance. When I roll onto my back, taking the dark sheets with me, I search the room, but I am alone.

For a moment, it feels a little like he was a figment of my imagination.

I should ache from the way he used my body. I should feel the lingering effects of it. All that remains is the golden shimmer of my skin.

But Hell is real and the bright goldenrod yellow of Zuriel's shroud lays over a chair that looks like it's been burnt to a crisp.

He's gone, and my dress .... I look up and watch it flutter and float high above. I won't be able to retrieve it.

Slipping from the bed, I pluck up that shroud and slip it over my shoulders. It's warm and soft as silk and it clings to me everywhere my skin has been painted gold.

It has slits for his wings and drags behind me, but I pull the hood up over my head, hook the trailing hem over my arm and hurry to find my sister. I want to be back before he returns.

I would have sworn we were in a tower, but when I step out of the arched doorway, the hall in front of me is flat.

Bare feet in cool water, I don't deviate from the hallway I started on until I have no choice. Pausing, I listen only long enough to hear the crashing sound again and I turn toward it.

Even if it doesn't lead me to Keres, *someone* is there. I'll keep myself hidden until I know who.

It takes forever before I find my way to the edge of Zuriel's cathedral. Beyond the long waterfall: red tiles and hot air, and somewhere... my younger, far braver sister.

I leap over that channel once more. Higher this time, so those shadowy hands can't reach me.

It is hotter than I remember, and the floor stings at my bare feet.

I do what I can to ignore it as I hurry through the halls, following the sounds, but when they lead me down a curving stairway with walls close on each side, I know it's wrong.

Dread prickles at my skin, icy cold against the heat radiating from below and I turn back.

Too late.

I lose my footing as the steps crumble and there's nothing to grab hold of as I fall out of the Devil's palace into the loose, sharp rocks of the wasteland that surrounds it.

Those stones skitter away from me like crabs and I push to my feet taking in the hellscape around me with my heart in my throat.

This was a misstep I hadn't imagined possible.

Hell stretches out in front of me for an eternity.

Shrieks and screams fill the air, flooding my senses and making me dizzy.

High overhead, dark masses swoop and swirl... demons

that travel on wind and hot air. They drop into the masses and pull the damned up with them, rending them into pieces and littering the burning soil with their remains.

And there are so many of the damned to choose from.

They look at me with eyeless faces and mouths gaping in silent screams and they start toward me, shackled hands and feet slowing their progress. But there's no way to get back up to that open archway.

I step back, looking for some escape at either side, but there's nothing but the damned in front of me and the craggy wall behind me.

And when I can't back up any further, a shadow descends from above me, dark wings, dark body, a flaming sword in his hand.

Zuriel lands in the loose rocks in front of me and the damned shamble backward, away from the arc of that sword.

His wings fan out, extending so far, they block me like an enormous feathered shield.

Blue flames lick at the blade and he says something in the heavenly language I don't understand that sends them stumbling away to a "safe" distance.

"You are not where you are supposed to be," he says to me, back still turned. "You are a flame that lures them."

"I fell."

"You wandered too close to the edge."

"I know." I swallow back the last of my fears. He's here. I'm safe. "I'm sorry."

He heaves a sigh and his shoulders lose their tension, his wings flutter and settle back into place. And when he finally turns to me, dozens of golden eyes reflect my face.

Even though they don't move, I know they sweep over me from head to toe.

"You almost damned yourself, Thea."

He steps close and I gasp as he snatches the shroud away from me, slinging it over to cover him once more. My shoulder touches the stone behind me and I gasp again as it burns me, lurching away from it and into his arms.

"If they had touched you, you would have joined them and not even I could have saved you."

"But you're here." Relief mixes with lust and I melt against him, holding tight to his arms. "I'm safe when I'm with you."

I'm at peace when I'm with him.

I reach up, sliding my hand around his neck and pull him down to me, kissing him, but he pulls back. "Don't start something you won't want to finish."

"I want to finish it." I swallow back the lump that forms in my throat after I've said it. "I'm not supposed to want any of this. But I want you."

"You want me to tale you, here?" He asks, head tipping so that the shroud skims to the side and I can see the glimmer of those golden eyes. "I should claim you. I should fuck you for all the demons and the damned to see. So they know you are mine. And if you should fall into the wastes again, they will flee from you the way they flee from my sword."

"Yes. Do it."

Zuriel lifts me and pulls me down fully on a single stroke.

The pain is sharp, but it disappears a moment later and he presses me against the rough wall. Those stones burn at my skin and... I like it.

I like everything he does to me.

We're both fallen in our own ways.

"I want to see your face." He doesn't fight me when I

push the shroud back to hang behind him like a hood and I see myself reflected back in all of his eyes.

For the first time—in a very long time—I feel beautiful beneath someone else's gaze.

The sting of my burning flesh fades as pleasure notches higher. There could be a million of the damned here to watch us and I wouldn't notice. *He* is all my being knows.

His hand breaks the rock beside us, fingers digging into the stone and his mouth presses into a hard line.

"Tell me you are mine, Thea. Tell me you're mine to have and to hold."

"I'm yours."

"Tell me you'll honour and obey."

They're vows I remember, vows that had withered and died above but that could be so easy to keep for him. "Yes."

He kisses me and his tongue fills me, fucking my throat in the same rhythm that his cock fills my pussy.

It's too much. *He* is too much. And still, I want more.

I come on a broken cry, before burying my face in the crook of his neck and then collapse into his arms.

He holds me tightly to him, lips dotting my skin with kisses and he whispers. "Wrap your legs around me."

I do, still fully impaled on him and then I pull myself upright, to see the wastes beneath us, spreading out in every direction. There *are* millions of damned souls toiling in the unyielding, fiery rock.

"That is no place for you." He says as he carries me back into the Devil's palace and back to the cool blue corridors of his cathedral.

He lays me on a divan and makes me let him go, but his grip moves to my hips and I gasp and arch against him, moaning his name as he fucks me again, as he chases that orgasm he didn't get outside.

"I will not tell you that you cannot explore, starlight. But if I lose you because of it, the Devil will not be the one who torments you for eternity."

He withdraws from me, pulling me down and he strokes his cock once, twice more. I close my eyes as he comes across my face and over my lips. I tip my head back as it flows along my jaw and down my neck.

He doesn't need to claim me anymore. I'm his.

But I won't tell him to stop.

Holy Water

Zuriel pulls the shroud back over his head and even though I don't like it, I don't complain.

He lifts me up and I snuggle close to the soft fabric, dozing as he takes me back to the bedroom I've come to think of as *ours*.

A round marble basin sits at one edge of the room, large enough we could both fit in it comfortably, but he doesn't join me when he sets me inside.

From within the shroud, in a pocket I neither saw nor felt, he pulls free a pitcher that seems to be made of the same blue glass as the windows overhead.

And when he tips it, it's not water that pours from that pitcher, it's pure light, but it fills the bath just the same.

Sitting on the floor beside the basin, he lifts up one of my feet and begins to wash the red and cracked skin. I hadn't realised how bad they were, but the light he bathes me in washes away any trace of those burns and marks. He works his way up my legs, smoothing the scar from my knee surgery and then his thumb draws along the c-section scar and it disappears too. He washes away all the damage of my mortal life, but the gold stains from his cum remain.

But I'm not the only one the wasteland affected. "Your feathers are singed."

He looks at the wing I point to with a dripping finger and shakes it, ruffling the feathers and ash falls from them like snow. When he stills his wings again, there's no sign of the burns that were once there.

I hold my hand out to him and after a moment's pause, he slips the shroud from his shoulders, setting it aside. He joins me in the basin, moving me until I rest against him, head on his shoulder, his wings creating a sort of canopy over us.

We laze there for what feels like hours. The light never cools, and my thoughts follow a tangled path.

"The man I killed is out there, among the damned, isn't he?"

"Yes."

"Do you know which one he is?"

"No."

He doesn't ask me, but I'm compelled to tell him. I need for him to know....

"I cleaned houses for a living. Niro—I mean my ex. I'm not invoking his name. He asked me to clean his friend's place at a discount. When I did, I found a trophy case. Not that it was obvious that was what it was. But there were little tells, and I went home with my suspicions and I looked at the reports I could get my hands on and when I *knew* for certain what he had done.... The next time I went to clean, I took what I needed with me.

"Mix the right household cleaners together and you can make chloroform. I was already parked in the garage so he was easy enough to move."

"And then you killed him."

I nod. "I drowned him. There was a shallow creek near his home. But it was deep enough. I weighed him down and rolled him into the water right as he regained consciousness. I watched as he flailed and splashed."

"You wanted him to suffer."

"Yes."

"And now he's dead and his victims were found and their families have closure."

"What's one murder against however many more he would have committed?"

"I believe the proper response is to ask why you didn't let the Earthly authorities handle it?"

"He *was* 'the authorities.' I couldn't report him to himself or his friends."

I trail my fingers along the surface of the light. "I think my ex knew."

"You think he put you in the other man's path, hoping he would kill you too?"

"Maybe." I remember his face too well. "After I'd done it, it felt like he looked at me differently. Like he knew. And maybe he did. He wasn't shocked when they found his body. I think he told the officers I did it."

"You survived."

"I was too old to be a target."

"Had he killed you, it would have given me a reason to stay in Heaven."

I swallow the coil of absurdity that catches in my throat. "I'm just a sinner. Your choice to stay or return shouldn't involve me."

"You're more than that. You're worth—"

"You can't know that."

"I know enough." His hand coasts down my arm. "I

know that you're strong and you're brave and you understand the need for justice in a world that cunt made unnecessarily cruel."

"I'm no one."

"If that was true, I wouldn't have been drawn to you as I was." He lifts a handful of water and pours it out again. "You were strong enough to leave him."

"If I had stayed with him, I wouldn't be here."

"If you had stayed with him, you would have suffered a different hell." He turns my head toward him and his tongue —his *tongues*... there are at least a half dozen of the black, tendrils that reach out—draw across his lips. "I am glad you chose this Hell, Thea, my star."

"I'd lived in that other hell for too long... So I left and I bought a dress and I waited for All Hallows Eve to come. But I didn't expect you."

Baptism by Fire

I lose all track of time as Zuriel makes love to me in every corner of the blue-limned cathedral I've come to think of as his home.

Days have passed, whether they add up to months, or even years, I can't begin to comprehend. I don't want or need to count.

Slowly... ever so slowly, I wonder if I need to find Keres at all. My sister is precisely where she wanted to be. She looked happy on the Devil's dance floor and I trusted Zuriel when he confirmed it.

He still wears his shroud when he isn't inside of me in one way or another, but when we are together, as we are now, bound in this most primal way, he hides nothing of himself from me.

"Stay with me," he says, tracing his hand up my leg, over my hip and waist to cup my breast.

"I'm not going anywhere." *Yet.* Eventually, I'll have to join the hordes toiling outside.

"You *are* a sinner. But I can fix it so you never have to fear falling into the fiery pit. You'll never join the hoards that toil in the scorched wastes outside."

I don't know if I trust that's possible. "How?"

"I've chosen banishment from Heaven." He kisses the tip of my nose. "I questioned the cunt too many times, wondering whether my friend wasn't right. So, she sent me here to join him."

His fingers trail down my throat. "You're going to Hell when you die, Thea."

"I know."

"But if you don't die...."

"Is the holy grail hidden somewhere in these walls?"

His smile twists and I wish it was followed by a laugh.

"Let me baptise you again. Not in water, but in my cum. You'll have to let me gild every inch of you." He traces the line of where my normal skin meets the gold. "It will mean you can never go back to the world above. You'll be stuck here for the rest of eternity and you'll be mine."

His.

I belonged to someone once. "What happens when you grow tired of me?"

"This is not an offer I make lightly."

No, it isn't. There is a pain in the dark glimmer of his eyes.

And I'm tired. I *want* to stay here, with him where nothing hurts unless I want it to.

More than that—even if I shouldn't—I trust that he won't abandon me.

"I want to stay with you." I lick my lips and take one more breath before I say. "Make me yours."

I take his hands and he supports me as I go to my knees in front of him.

"Are you certain this is what you want, sweet starlight?"

"There's nothing left for me there."

"There is everything left for you there." He turns my wrist, flicking open the locket.

The four hearts fall to make a four-leaf clover. The pictures are of my children when they were still children.

"They're grown. They have their own lives to live without me." I close the locket. "I keep their memories. Their futures don't belong to me."

Pushing the sides of his shroud away from his hips, I run my hands up his darkly corded, smooth-as-marble thighs and slip my fingers around his cock.

His wings shiver with my first stroke.

Zuriel is perfection, standing before me.

I stroke him and lick my lips, wanting to suck his cock and not wanting to waste a drop at the same time.

"Will you take me, Thea? As I am and as I will be, yours forever from this day forth?" His hips move in a frenzied rhythm and his lids droop.

"I will. For better or worse."

His smile is soft and so severe. "Neither God nor death will part us when you are mine as well."

An angelic curse crosses his lips and he takes hold of my hair, pulling me back and angling my head up to him. He kisses me so deeply, I almost forget what we're doing. And then his cum pours onto me.

His hand wraps around mine and he eases my fingers free... even though he hasn't finished.

Moving around me, he uses more plucked feathers to paint my skin. "You are lovely, my golden star."

When he draws me to my feet, I see myself in his eyes. I'm "dipped", but not *covered* in gold.

"I'll give you what I've offered when you've asked for it one more time." He presses a finger to my lips to keep me from doing so now. "I need to be certain that you won't regret this."

I won't, but I purse my lips beneath his finger, and when he draws his hand down me, the blue dress falls into place over my body once more.

At a distance it might look as though I'm wearing an off the shoulder golden shirt beneath the dress. The golden streaks that line my chin and throat and the stains that cover my forehead and run beneath my eyes like permanent tears give it away.

He pulls his shroud back over his head, hiding the reflection. "Go to your sister. I'll only intervene if you get into trouble again."

"Will you punish me for it?"

"Is it punishment you crave?"

I crave him.

And he knows it.

Fallen Angel's Folly

The halls feel brighter and warmer than the last time I was here. Like the gold on my skin might truly be metal, reflecting and focusing the heat, wanting to drip from me instead of sweat.

I hold the skirt up—stars spilling down the fabric from my fingers—as I walk, turning the opposite direction of the ones that had lead me to fall into the pit.

Fluttering in the rib vaults, utterly out of place, a dove flies ahead of me, its white feathers acting as a beacon.

That is how I find her.

Keres lays on a chaise, watching the mortal world through a dark mirror and plucking withered black grapes from a stem. They ripen in her fingers... her red-stained fingers.

The Devil, thank God, is nowhere to be found.

"Keres," I whisper her name—even though I don't think I need to—and she sits bolt upright.

"Thea?"

We blink at each other for a moment and I say all that I can manage. "You look like a cartoon devil."

She snorts a laugh and stands. "And you look like you've been playing with Midas."

But neither of us are completely covered.

She stands, a dress of smoke coalescing around her.

Her gaze coasts up me. "Your hair!"

I twist a strand in my fingers. "I dyed it after you left."

"I love it." She hugs me and then steps back. "But what are you doing here?"

"I divorced Niro."

"So you danced." Understanding washes over her face, quickly replaced by confusion. "But that was eight months ago, why are you still here? Oh dear, mom must have gone to pieces waiting for you to come back."

"I wasn't a saint."

Her smile fades and she takes a step back. "But you haven't been toiling in the wastes."

"No, I—"

There is a faint rumble and the scent of brimstone before the Devil fades into view from the shadows.

"You should not be here." His eyes—no whites or irises, just dozens of black pupils crowded together—shift as he looks over my skin. "And yet, there's nowhere else you could be."

The lord of darkness is bigger than my angel. He steps out with claw-like feet, dark fur covering most of his body and horns. But he only has two wings.

Still, I flinch back from him, colliding with the hard chest of Zuriel. My angel wraps his arm around my waist, holding me tight to him.

"She is *precisely* where she should be."

The Devil's strange eyes slide from me up to lock on Zuriel. "You took her from the dance and have been hiding her ever since?"

"You of all angels can't begrudge for wanting to keep her to myself until she was ready to forsake all others."

"And is she?"

"Yes." He didn't ask me, but he should have.

The Devil turns back to me. "Are you a family of fools then?"

I glance at Keres who shakes her head with a soft smile on her lips, looking up at her Devil.

And with Zuriel at my back, I feel as though I have more spine than I used to.

"My sister came to Hell to find you. I have chosen my angel. Are we fools? Or conquerors?"

Keres lifts her hand to cover her laughter and I hear her say, "My sister certainly isn't a coward."

The Devil makes a sound that might be disapproval. "You wear his marks, and yet... he is the one who has been claimed."

Zuriel's hand tightens on my waist. "You should know how that feels, Lucifer."

The Devil looks down at my sister and I would swear he softens.

"Your halo is gone." His chest heaves and he looks at us. "I told you, you could stay—"

"And unlike the cunt upstairs, you don't go back on your word."

"I do not. And if she is yours and you are hers, she of course is included in that invitation."

"We will leave you to each other. And I will ensure that Thea knows where your private sanctuaries are, should she go wandering."

He draws me away and Keres calls after us. "We are going to have a long talk."

I don't know which of us it's meant for. But it doesn't matter, we'll have plenty of time in our eternities.

Eternally Damned, Eternally Devoted

Zuriel leads me back through the halls, but this time, when we reach the channel that separates his part of the Devil's palatial cathedral, there is a bridge to keep the souls from snatching at my feet.

He doesn't take me back to the room we've spent so much time in. He leads me, instead, to the altar where first I promised to obey him.

Between one step and the next, my dress slips through me, hanging in the centre of the aisle as though worn by a ghost.

It crumples to the floor, pooling in blue silk when Zuriel lifts me back onto that altar. "You are mine, aren't you, starlight? Mine to claim, mine to keep. I've fucked you in front of the damned." He pushes my legs wide. "Now I'll take you in front of God and all her hypocritically voyeuristic angels."

He lifts himself up on those dark wings and kneels on the altar, adjusting my hips so that he can ease himself into me.

"Let God watch. Let her know she's lost you. The cunt never deserved you in the first place."

The shroud falls back as he scoops his hands beneath me and I wrap my arms around his neck. I don't care if God is watching. I don't care about anything but him.

And when I kiss him, rocking my hips to meet each thrust, no one else exists.

His lips coast over my cheek, my jaw. He leans me back so that he can kiss his way down my throat and sternum as his cock moves within me.

This is an act of worship.

If I wasn't already in Hell, I'm sure I would have been smited.

What kind of woman can make an angel treat her like she's God?

Me.

The warmth of his cum fills me, burning through me like a fever and I tighten around him, my body knowing it wants to keep every ounce of him I can.

"Take me, Thea." The command in his voice zings through me the way all the others have, and yet, it burns brighter. "Conquer me."

I can't do anything as his thumb digs into my clit. He swirls it and the pressure releases from me on a scream that rattles dust and ash from the vaulting, like snowflakes tumbling down.

My orgasm burns through me, hotter than the fires in the pit, and I drag his face to mine, kissing him as I shake and jerk through the tidal wave of it. My nails dig into his skin and I want to crawl inside of him. All I can do is ride out the sensations that threaten to drown me.

He pulls back from me, but this time, instead of releasing the last of his cum onto my skin, he pulls a chalice from beneath the statue of him and pours that bright, golden cum into it.

It glows more brightly than the light he washed me in after I'd fallen out into the wasteland. Like molten gold inside it, I lick my lips, wanting to consume him.

"This choice is yours to make. There will be no consequences if you have changed your mind."

But I haven't. I take the cup from him, and pour a line across my breasts, taking a feather from his hand and using it the way he has before, painting the places his cum doesn't flow on its own.

When I tip my face back and close my eyes, the rest of it slides from my forehead down to drip from my chin. It is Zuriel who uses that feather to paint me again. To—

I gasp when the last bit of my skin is covered. It feels as though the energy of a thousand light bulbs has burst through my skin and when I open my eyes, I can *see*.

The cathedral around us is still burnt and dark, but I can see what it once was. I can see the bright light streaming through and the smooth pillars, their stones unpitted.

I can see Zuriel, even though he still wears his shroud.

He watches me with a soft smile, all of his eyes fixed on me.

"You shine so brightly... truly my star." He reaches out to brush my hair away from my eyes. "I love you. I loved you from the moment you first looked at me and were unafraid."

"I knew you were the one I was made for when you loved me the first time and now that you are mine for eternity, I will continue to love you with every fibre of my being."

"I love you too. I hadn't realised that what I'd felt before was something too shallow to be called love. That was a puddle. This is an ocean."

He pulls a handful of the golden feathers from beneath his shroud and when he releases them, they hang like fabric. Wrapping them around me he turns me until they cover me, like the dress I had once worn.

Drawing me close, he kisses me, and spins me down the aisle. We dance into the darkness to find our own Heaven in this Hell.

About Dalia

Dalia Davies fell into monster romance, almost by accident, and loves it here. She drinks her weight in tea every day and has been told on numerous occasions that she "knows too much".

She pairs old gods, monsters, and aliens with human women who get exactly what they want and maybe a little more than they came for.

Brought up on fairytales read while hiding in the back stacks of her small-town library and sneaking in creature features at friends' homes, she always wanted a way to meld two fantasies into one. When not writing, she plays the banjo poorly, dreams of traveling the world, and avoids large crowds and loud noises.

Living in the southwestern US, she lets the outside heat permeate her stories and hopes they leave you panting.

Find more info and sign up for the newsletter at www.daliadavies.com

Become a Patron

For early access, exclusive stories, sneak peeks at art, and quarterly mail, at patreon.com/daliadavies

Also by Dalia Davies

Devil's Dance

The Dame & The Devil

The Flame & The Fallen

The Halo & The Heathen

Valley of the Old Gods

Railed by the Easter Bunny

Banging the Easter Bunny

Railed by the Krampus

Railed at the Bacchanal

Railed by the Reaper

Books as Ava Lunaria

Paranormal Mates of Erinbren University

Seized by the Pack

A Taste For Blood

Alone with the Alpha

Surrender to the Night

Stealing my Father's Pack

One Month with a Wolf

Coven of Curiosities

Scarlette Mathis

Blue Moon Lover

Blood Moon Huntress

Midwinter Mistress

Elaria Mason

Witch's Bane

Crossing the Coven

The Wolf Wife

VANQUISHING

Love's First Bite

Twice Bitten

Books as Andi Simms

A Taste of Something Wicked

Fate at Fault

Fair Bargain

With this Vow

All Fun & Games

At Summer's End

Like & Sub

Nine Two Five

Print Omnibus books 1-4

Print Omnibus books 5-8

Made in the USA
Monee, IL
02 December 2023